Jeet and Fudge

FOREVER FRIENDS

by Amandeep S. Kochar
with Candy Rodó

PUBLISHING
pawprintspublishing.com

Book and Cover Design by Maureen O'Connor
illustrated by Weaverbird Interactive
Edited by Bobbie Bensur and Alison A. Curtin

English Paperback ISBN: 978-1-22318-346-6
English eBook ISBN: 978-1-22318-347-3

Published by Paw Prints Publishing
PawPrintsPublishing.com

Jeet lives in California.
He was adopted when
he was small.

His parents, his Bebbe and
Bapu, love him very much.

Jeet and his family moved to a new town. He misses his friends. He is feeling a bit lonely and sad.

"Are you okay, Jeet?" asks Mom.

"Let's go for a walk!" she says.
"It will help."
"Okay," says Jeet.

On their walk...
They run down the street.

They skip stones on the lake.

They visit the outdoor market.

They also share ice cream with extra fudge!

But, after all the fun, Jeet is still sad.
"You know, Jeet?" says Mom. "Soon
you will make new friends. I'm sure!"
"I hope so," says Jeet.

Suddenly, they hear dogs barking. Jeet loves dogs!

"It's coming from this animal shelter!" says Jeet.
"Can we go in, Bebbe?"

"We can volunteer here," says Mom. "It's a good way to serve our community. And, a great way to make friends."

"Yes," says Jeet, "I want to serve!"

Mom smiles and goes to speak with the manager.
Jeet stays to play with the dogs.

There are so many!
Some are big.
Some are small.

"Hello, little one!" Jeet says.
The happy dog licks his face.
And licks.
And licks!

"You are so sweet! I will call you Fudge!"

Evening comes and it's time to go. "Bye, Fudge! See you tomorrow!"

Yub
ANIMAL

When they get home,
Jeet can't wait to tell Dad
all about his new friend.

"Her name is Fudge! She is awesome!"
"Wonderful!" replies Dad.

That night, Jeet falls asleep
happy. He dreams of Fudge.
In his dream, they play together
at home.

The next morning, Jeet gets up early. He runs downstairs. "Let's go to the shelter!" he says. Mom giggles. "Breakfast first!"

It's a warm, sunny day.
Jeet plays with Fudge in
the shelter's backyard.
They run.
They play fetch.
They jump!
Time goes too fast!

On the way home, Jeet says, "You gave me a forever-home. Can we give Fudge a forever-home?"
"We'll see," says Mom.

At home, Jeet tries to convince Dad.

"Bapu, can we adopt Fudge?"

"A dog is a lot of work. Are you ready?" asks Dad.

"Yes, I am!" replies Jeet.

Jeet is not sure he's convinced his parents.
He sure hopes so!

That night, he dreams his far-away friends visit. In the dream, Jeet has new friends, too.
They all play with Fudge!
His favorite friend of all.

Sometimes, dreams come true.
The next morning...

A surprise!
Fudge now has a forever-home.
And Jeet has Fudge.
His forever-friend.

For many children, animal companions have a positive impact on their lives.

- Pets become safe outlets for children to share their feelings, both positive and negative. They combat loneliness and make great companions!

- Pets aid in a child's social-emotional health through the development of empathy, respect, and loyalty.

- Pets help children become more responsible and reliable.

- Pets – especially dogs that need walks and playtime – help keep kids active.

- Studies show that playing with a pet reduces the levels of the stress hormone cortisol in the body.

- Pets build confidence and self-esteem through their unconditional love and acceptance.

- Pets bond families by encouraging more time spent together, as well as cooperation to fulfill shared responsibilities.

- Pets teach children about the cycle of life.

- Find shelters in your area where you can volunteer to help animals or to adopt pets. You can also contact humanesociety.org and aspca.org for information on volunteering opportunities and pet adoptions.

- **Did You Know?** Jeet and his family are first generation Indian-Americans, and they are also Sikh. Sikhism originated in India, but is now practiced worldwide. Sikhs believe that humans and the rest of the natural world are harmonious and should be respected equally. Therefore, animals are very important and valuable. Working hard, sharing resources, and participating in community service are particularly important in Sikhism.